A VERY GRUMPY VALENTINE'S DAY

WOLF VALLEY: A VERY GRUMPY HOLIDAY
BOOK 1

SHAW HART

 Created with Vellum

WANT A FREE BOOK?

You can grab Sweets **Here.**
Check out my website, www.shawhart.com for more free books!

This Ex-Army Ranger has met his match...

Mira:

Getting out of my parents' house was meant to be a chance for me to spread my wings.

Instead, I seem to have picked up a new babysitter.

Townes Monroe is grumpy and bossy.

Every time I turn around, he's there.

The man seems to know exactly how to press my buttons.

I'm just not sure if that's a good thing or not.

Townes:

I've never wanted to be tied down.

Not until I see Mira Lane.

She obviously needs someone to look after her, and that person is going to be me.

I just need to get her on board with that plan.

With Valentine's Day coming up, I know that this is my chance to win over my girl and finally make her mine.

I just hope that my plan is good enough.

ONE

Mira

"THANKS FOR STAYING LATE," Saffron says as she sniffles.

"It's no problem," I assure her. "I hope that you feel better soon. Now go get some rest."

She smiles weakly as she gathers her things and heads for the door. I turn back to the bookstore once she's gone and look around at what I have left to do tonight.

The Shelf Indulgence Bookstore is empty at this time of night. To be fair, most of the shops in Wolf Valley are closed by now, so there's not much reason for people to be out. The only other store that's open is the other shop I work at, the Wet and Wild adult toy store.

I grab the Clorox wipes and start wiping down every surface that Saffron may have touched today. Disinfecting like this is second nature to me. I was sick a lot as a kid and teenager, and I can remember my mom wiping down every surface in our house nearly every day. It's hard to tell if my mom was doing that because she was worried about someone else getting sick or if it was her own OCD that made her do that.

Growing up in my house was kind of rough. My mom was a germaphobe with untreated OCD who was afraid of everything. She never wanted to leave the house and hated to let me leave the house either. I would come home from school and have to immediately take a shower and change my clothes. I used to have to wash my hands so often that they would be red and raw.

I was isolated in that house. The only person that I had to talk to was my mom, and as you can imagine, that wasn't a whole lot of fun.

When I was a little older and started driving, I tried to gain a bit more freedom and independence. That didn't go over well.

I was the weird girl at school, so I didn't have many friends. Even if I did, it's not like I could have gone out or done stuff with them. I couldn't have had them over to my house either.

I made a plan when I was seventeen to save up as much money as I could and get out of there. I worked at a grocery store throughout high school and saved up every penny. I didn't have anything else to spend the money on since I was barely allowed out of the house.

When I turned twenty, I tried to convince my mom to go to therapy to get some help. I had brought up the idea before, but kind of vaguely, and she had always just kind of brushed me off. That time was different though. Instead of ignoring me or brushing my suggestion off, she blew up at me, telling me that nothing was wrong with her and insisting that she didn't need therapy or any help at all.

I ended up leaving home the very next day and I haven't

been back since. I have no plans on going back either. It's been two years, and I haven't heard from her once.

I try not to think about my mom because it hurts too much. I want to focus on the positive, which is the fact that I got out, that I'm supporting myself, that I have friends and my freedom. I'm still trying to find myself and see what I like. Still, every now and then, I wonder what my mom is doing and if she misses me.

I push those thoughts aside and finish unboxing the newest shipment of books. It's almost closing time, so I set them on the counter to log into the system and put them on the shelves tomorrow. I leave a note for Saffron next to the books in case she's feeling better tomorrow and decides to come to work. Then, I gather my things and get ready to lock up.

As I close the door and pocket my keys, I'm not surprised to see Townes leaning against the side of the bookstore.

Excitement and arousal bubble up inside of me, and I try to force it down. Townes is hot, but he's also overbearing and a bit of a grump. He's always trying to do things for me, and I both love and hate it. Either way, ever since I moved to Wolf Valley five months ago, I seem to have picked up a new babysitter.

At first, I liked his attention. Being in a new town and all alone was kind of scary, but he always made me feel safe. Then he started trying to take over for me. He was always grabbing my groceries before I could, carrying boxes into the bookstore when I was doing inventory, opening water bottles for me, and just generally hovering around me.

"Mira," Townes says in his deep voice.

"Shadow," I reply, using the nickname I gave him when he first started popping up.

"How was work?" He asks, ignoring the nickname.

"Good."

"I didn't think that you closed tonight," he says, and I side-eye him.

"How did you get my schedule?"

"It's the same every week," he points out.

"Saffron wasn't feeling well," I tell him, and he frowns.

"What about you?" He asks, reaching over to feel my forehead with the back of his hand.

I get a flashback to my mom doing that to me and I flinch, stepping away from him.

"I'm fine."

"You look tired. Come on, I'll buy you some soup at the diner and then walk you home."

He starts heading towards Nosh, the diner a few blocks away, and I roll my eyes. Townes has a habit of ordering me around and expecting me to do as he bids. I never do.

"I'm going home, but you have fun," I call, turning and heading towards my apartment.

"Wait," he says as he grabs my arm.

I don't know how he can move so quickly or so quietly. The guy is huge, but I feel like he's always sneaking up on me.

"Are you really feeling alright?" He asks again, his hand going to my forehead, and I sigh as I let him take my temperature. "You look kind of pale."

"I'm fine," I tell him again, pulling out of his grip.

He frowns down at me and I turn and start to walk faster towards my apartment. I only live two blocks from the bookstore, so the walk is over quickly.

Townes falls into step beside me, easily matching my steps with his long legs.

"Did you eat enough today?" He asks, and I roll my eyes.

He asks me this question a lot. It seems like he's always trying to feed me. I'm already curvy and plus size, so I definitely don't need the extra calories, but that doesn't stop him from trying.

A few guys stumble out of the Wolf Pack Bar on the corner, and Townes moves closer to me, pressing me closer to the building next to me as we pass them. I glance over at Townes as the guys laugh and push each other as they trip and stumble in the opposite direction. Townes is glaring at them, watching until they turn the corner and disappear from view.

"Down, boy," I joke, and he frowns at me.

He's been frowning at me a lot lately. Maybe he's getting tired of me.

That thought hurts, and I clear my throat and look up at my apartment building.

"You shouldn't be walking home alone," he tells me.

We have this conversation about once a week, and I sigh.

"I never do. You're always there, shadow."

"It's not safe for you to be out here after dark by yourself," he continues, acting like I didn't say anything.

"Uh huh."

"I'm serious, Mira."

"I'm *fine*," I stress, and I don't need to look at him to know that he's frowning again.

My steps slow automatically as I dig my keys out of my purse. I turn towards Townes to say goodnight, and my breath stalls in my lungs as I see the look in his eyes.

There's heat and longing in their blue depths. He's been staring at me like that when he walks me home for the past few weeks, and I keep waiting to see if he's going to kiss me or make some kind of move.

"Good night, Mira," Townes says quietly, and I nod.

"Night."

I try not to let my disappointment show as I unlock the door and head up the stairs to my apartment.

"Lock the door," he calls through the wooden front door, and I want to scream.

He's always telling me to do the most basic of tasks. It's like he thinks I'm an idiot or incapable of taking care of myself in any way.

I ignore him as I let myself into my apartment. I live in a tiny one-bedroom apartment above Manci's Pizza Parlor. The place always smells like tomatoes, garlic, and oregano, and I've found myself craving pizza more than ever since I started living here.

I toss my things down on the kitchen counter and sigh as I look around the cramped space. I shower and get ready for bed. As I crawl onto the mattress, an image of Townes tonight flashes behind my eyes. He's staring down at me with that longing look in his dark eyes, and a shiver of lust rushes through me.

As I lay down and close my eyes, I know that I'm going to dream of Townes again tonight.

TWO

Townes

I'M DISTRACTED two mornings later, looking out the windows of the Nosh Diner for any sign of Mira walking by.

"Earth to Townes," my best friend, Xavier, says, and I blink, turning back to our table.

I'm having breakfast with my friends, and I'm meant to be catching up with everyone, but all I can think about is a certain curvy brunette.

"Sorry, what were you saying?" I ask, trying to focus on my friends.

"We were asking what your plans were for the weekend," Foster says.

I grab my coffee and peek back at the windows to see if I can spot any sign of Mira.

"Um, I'm not sure yet," I tell them.

"Maybe you'll have a date," Xavier says with a pointed look.

Xavier knows about my crush on Mira and has been pushing me to make a move or ask her out for weeks now. He just got together with his girlfriend, Olive, right before Christmas, and now that he's in love, it's like he can't wait for me to be with someone too.

To be fair, having someone like that does look nice. Xavier went from being a complete grumpy loner to a complete grumpy loner who just happens to be in love with the curvy baker in town. Now he gets out more, mainly because Olive wants to do something, and he would just do anything to make her happy.

That's how I already feel about Mira. I mean, I wait outside in the freezing cold at least three times a week just to walk her home and be around her for five minutes. She's all that I can think about, all that I dream or fantasize about.

Xavier calls it a crush, but what I feel for Mira is so much more than that. She's it for me. I've known that since the moment that I laid eyes on her. I had frozen right in my tracks and just stared as she walked down the sidewalk and disappeared into the bookstore. I ended up following her in just to get another look at her. Then I went back the next day, the next week, and the next week.

I've tried talking to her and flirting with her, and it's gotten me nowhere. She doesn't seem to pick up on the fact that I like her or that I'm trying to flirt with her. She's been keeping me at arm's length. Sometimes, I feel like maybe I even annoy her, but then there are days when it seems like she might like me too. It's those moments that keep giving me hope.

"Maybe," I lie to Xavier, and I see him and Foster share a look.

Foster is equally in love with his best friend, Lilliana. Xavier, Foster, and Ford grew up in Wolf Valley, and apparently, Foster has loved Lilliana since they were kids. She felt the same way, and it took her coming back to town for them to finally admit how they felt for each other.

I don't want that. I don't want to spend years pining for Mira. I need her, and I want to be with her.

"What about you guys?" I ask.

Ford, Foster's twin brother and the owner of the Nosh Diner, heads our way with our food, and I welcome the distraction.

"How's it going?" Ford asks, and I smile.

"Pretty good. What about you?"

"Staying busy," he says as he passes out the plates.

The door of the diner opens, and Cameron rushes in wearing a waitress uniform.

"Sorry that I'm late, boss!" She calls to Ford, and he just nods, his eyes glued to her.

"Dial it back, brother," Foster whispers to Ford, and he snaps out of his stupor and turns back to our table.

"You two should form a group," Xavier says with a laugh.

"Yeah, the lovestruck grumps," Foster adds. "Ransom could join too."

"Shut up," I grumble.

Ford just rolls his eyes and heads back behind the counter, and I dig into my breakfast. Foster and Xavier are busy eating too so I take the moment to look out the window again.

Mira still hasn't walked by, and I frown. I know that she had to work at the bookstore today and should have gone by before now.

Could she have overslept? Is she alright? I should go check on her.

The door of the diner opens, and Saffron rushes in and

up to the counter to grab the to-go cup of coffee that Ford is filling up for her. She thanks him and turns to rush back out but I stop her as she walks past our table.

"Hey," I say, stopping her before she can leave. "Where's Mira?"

"Oh, she's sick this morning. I feel so bad. She probably caught what I had," Saffron says, looking sad.

I push to my feet, and she steps back, staring at me with wide eyes. Foster and Xavier don't look surprised as I grab my wallet and throw down some bills.

"I'll see you later," I tell them, and they wave as I head for the door.

I hop in my truck and head down the two blocks to Mira's apartment. The lights are off when I look up at the windows, and worry starts to gnaw at me as I hop out of my truck and hurry over to the door.

I ring the buzzer and wait impatiently. Finally, the intercom crackles, and I lean closer.

"Hello?" She croaks.

"Mira, it's me. Let me in," I growl into the intercom.

"I'm fine, Townes. I just need to rest."

The intercom crackles like she turned it off, and I hit the button again.

"Go away," she sighs when she answers again.

"Not a chance. I'm not going anywhere. Let me up or I'm just going to stand here all day and ring the buzzer."

"You can't order me around," she snaps, sounding more like herself.

"Wanna bet?" I snap.

The intercom remains silent, and I take a deep breath, trying to calm down.

"Mira, please let me in," I relent.

I would beg her for anything. I would get on my knees

and grovel for her to just look at me. I am clearly wrapped around her finger, and she doesn't even seem to realize it.

She sighs loud and long, but then the door buzzes and I push inside and take the stairs two at a time up to her door. She's leaning against the doorframe, looking pale and tired but still so beautiful.

"What are your symptoms?" I ask, already reaching to feel her forehead.

"I'm just tired and have a runny nose," she says, trying to push my hand away.

"What do you need?" I ask.

"Nothing. I just need to go back to bed," she insists.

"Give me your keys," I demand, and she glares up at me. "What? No."

"Give me your keys and you can go back to bed."

She groans but reaches over and grabs her keys. She drops them into my hand, and I smile at her.

"Get some rest."

She closes the door in my face, and I turn and jog back downstairs and over to my truck. The Wolf Valley Market isn't far, and I head there to grab her some things. I try to think about what would make me feel better. I've never taken care of anyone or had anyone take care of me, so I feel woefully unprepared in this moment.

I head down the first aisle and grab Mira some medicine, shower steamers, some Vitamin C gummies, and Kleenex. I pass by the produce and decide to make her soup too. I pull up a chicken noodle soup recipe and grab everything listed under the ingredients there. Before I head to the checkout, I grab some Gatorade and juices.

I pay and load all of the bags into my truck and then make the short drive back to Mira's apartment. She's asleep when I carry everything inside, so I line the medicine and everything else on the counter and then I get to work making the soup.

It's just after noon when she comes out of the bedroom, looking half asleep.

"I got you some things," I say, nodding towards the medicine and Kleenex.

"Thanks."

"And I made you some soup."

"You didn't have to do that," she insists, and I frown at her.

"I know. I wanted to. Now sit down. You need to eat."

She looks away from me, and I dig through her cabinets until I find her bowls and grab two. I ladle the soup into the bowls and pass her one. She hands me a spoon and we sit together on her couch, side by side, to eat.

We eat in silence, and I take Mira's bowl when she's done.

"Thanks again. I'm just going to go back to bed," she tells me.

"Okay. I'll be here."

"You can leave," she tries to argue, but I just shake my head.

"You should drink something. Do you need anything else?"

She heads over to the fridge and grabs a Gatorade, chugging half of it in one big gulp. She plops back down on the couch next to me and wraps herself up in the blanket that's draped over the back of the couch.

She doesn't say anything as she turns the TV on, leans her head back against the couch, and flips through the channels until she lands on some cooking show. She yawns, and I settle in next to her and pretend to watch the show when really I'm watching her.

We spend the rest of the day on her couch. Mira sleeps on and off. I keep passing her juice and Gatorade and set an alarm on my phone so that I can remember to give her medicine every six hours. We finish up the soup for dinner and then Mira puts a movie on and promptly falls asleep next to me.

At one point, her head falls onto my shoulder and I smile down at her sleeping form. I pull the blanket tighter around her and lie down next to her on the edge of the couch so that she can't roll off.

Then I turn the TV off and start to drift off too. Even though I have a crick in my neck from the couch armrest and my feet are hanging off the other end of the couch, it's still the best night's sleep of my entire life, all because I'm sleeping next to the woman of my dreams.

Mira

I WAKE up the next morning, my face smashed against Towne's chest. His arms are locked around me, holding me in place, and I take a moment to appreciate his strong, warm body pressed up against mine.

I peek up at him and see that he's still fast asleep, his slow, even breathing blowing the loose hair at my temples.

I hate to wake him up, but I really need to go to the bathroom. I try to wiggle out of his hold, but he only holds me tighter.

"Townes," I whisper, squirming against him a bit.

He blinks his eyes open and smiles down at me. His smile is so bright and open that I stop moving and just stare at him.

"Morning," he grumbles, burying his face in my neck.

His stubble tickles my skin, and I rub against him.

"Ah, morning," I say, my voice coming out low and breathy.

His hands grip my hips, and he tugs me against him. I can feel his erection digging into my stomach, and I gasp at the size and hardness that I feel.

"I... uh, I'm feeling better," I blurt, and Townes freezes against me.

I can feel his eyelashes brush against my neck as he blinks, seeming to wake up more. Then he clears his throat and pulls away from me slightly.

"That's good."

He sits up, and I scramble to sit up too. Then I stand and clear my throat.

"Thanks for taking care of me yesterday," I tell him, feeling shy all of a sudden.

"Anytime. I'll get out of your hair, but you should take it easy today," he says, and I nod.

I walk him over to the door and smile as he pauses.

"You know, if you really want to thank me, you could go out to dinner with me tonight."

I blink, freezing. I'm not sure how to respond. On the one hand, I want to go out with him, but is that a good idea? I'm still trying to figure out who I am, still trying to find my freedom and my place in this world. Townes could mess all of that up.

"I have work tonight at Wet and Wild," I tell him, and he nods.

"We'll go out tomorrow then."

I'm a little surprised that he's pushing this. He hasn't made a move on me in the months that I've known him. I wonder what's changed in the last twenty-four hours. Maybe he's just finally worked up the nerve to ask me out. Maybe this is the first opening that he's had with me.

"Alright," I say, trying to hide the excitement that I feel about going out on my very first date.

I never had the chance to date in high school, and once I moved out of my mom's house, I was too busy trying to survive and make ends meet to think about dating. Besides, I wanted to be alone. I wanted to explore and finally live my life. It's not like any guys were asking me out anyway.

"Tomorrow then. I'll pick you up at six."

I nod, not trusting my voice at that moment, and he smiles and then heads down the stairs. I watch him go and then turn back to my empty apartment. At some point last night, he did the dishes, and they're drying in the rack by the sink. My medicine and Kleenex and everything else that he bought for me are on the counter by my bedroom.

I head into the bedroom and then into the shower, washing off the sleep and sickness from my skin. I think about Townes, about how he surprised me by showing up yesterday.

Maybe it should have though. He's consistently been there for me, and I've never once asked him to be there for me. He's a good guy, someone that I trust. I would say that we're almost friends.

I just hope that tomorrow's date doesn't mess all of that up.

I finish my shower and get ready to go to work. I overslept this morning, and I need to be at the bookstore in an hour. I still need breakfast, so I head over to the Nosh Diner and grab a breakfast sandwich and coffee to go.

I pass by Xavier as I leave, and he smiles slightly at me as he holds the door open for me.

"Thanks," I say, and he just grunts in response.

I can see why the two of them are best friends. They're so alike. He must be grabbing them a late breakfast or something. Xavier and Townes own their own consulting firm.

They work in cyber security, and from what I've heard, they spend a lot of time staring at computer screens.

I hurry down the block and into Shelf Indulgence, waving at Saffron and her sister, Ginger, as I set my things down behind the front counter.

"Hey! How are you feeling?" Saffron asks me.

"A lot better. I was just kind of cold and run down yesterday, so it wasn't too serious."

"Good," Ginger says, sounding relieved.

"You would have thought it was with the way that Townes ran off when I told him that you weren't feeling well yesterday," Saffron says with a laugh.

"He what?" I ask, and she giggles.

"I went into Nosh to grab a coffee before I opened yesterday, and he stopped me and asked about you. I told him that you weren't working because you weren't feeling well, and he ran out of there like his butt was on fire," she tells me.

"Oh," I respond, not sure what else to say to that.

"He's so into you," Ginger says with a grin, and I smile weakly.

"I don't know about that."

"Oh, trust me, he is," Saffron says.

"I would love to have a big, strong, sexy man who followed me around like a puppy dog," Ginger adds, and jealousy spikes inside of me.

"What did you want me to work on today?" I ask, hoping to change the subject.

"I just need to finish up inventory and scan in those new books," Saffron says, and I nod and hurry back to the counter to get to work.

I can feel my friends' eyes on me as I go, but I ignore

them. I need to figure out how I feel about Townes before I start adding in other people's opinions.

I try to push thoughts of Townes out of my head as I grab the first book and get to work.

FOUR

Townes

"WHERE ARE YOU TAKING HER?" Xavier asks me, his voice sounding far away, and I know he must have put me on speakerphone.

"We're going over to Rosewood. She likes Mediterranean food, and there's supposed to be a good restaurant there."

"How do you know that she likes Mediterranean food?" He asks.

"She's always looking at recipes on her phone from that region."

"Stalker."

"Like you didn't know everything about Olive before you two started dating," I challenge him, and he doesn't respond.

"Good luck tonight," he tells me sincerely.

Xavier and I have been best friends since boot camp. We were both in the military together, but when Xavier got shot on our last deployment, we decided to get out. I followed him back to Wolf Valley since I didn't know where else to go.

I've never really had a home or a supportive family. Xavier and this place are the closest that I've ever gotten to either of those things. Until I met Mira, that is. Now, wherever she is feels like home.

"Thanks. I'll talk to you tomorrow," I say.

"See you."

We both hang up, and I take one last look at myself in the mirror, smoothing my hands over my button-down shirt and brush my dark hair back off my forehead. It's time for me to go pick her up, and I smile as I grab my keys and head out the door.

I bought a cabin a few miles from downtown Wolf Valley when we moved back here. It's a few miles away from Xavier's place and only ten minutes from Mira's apartment.

When I park outside of Mira's place, she's already out front, and I hurry to jump out of my Jeep and open the door for her.

"I would have come up to get you," I tell her with a smile as she heads my way.

"Oh, I had to drop something off at the bookstore for Saffron. I was just walking back and saw your Jeep so I waited."

I close her door, jog around to the driver's side, and climb behind the wheel. I smile over at her, taking her in. She's wearing a pair of dark, tight blue jeans and a maroon sweater. It's still chilly out today, and I wonder if she's warm enough. I reach over and crank up the heat as I pull away from the curb.

"You look beautiful," I tell her as we drive out of town and towards Rosewood.

"Thanks. I wasn't sure what we were doing or how dressed up I should be."

"You're perfect," I assure her.

I make the turn towards Rosewood and she stares with wide eyes out the window.

"Where are we going?" She asks, staring at the passing scenery.

"I found this restaurant in Rosewood that I think you'll like."

"I've never been to Rosewood," she mentions, and I smile.

I like the thought of showing her around and experiencing something for the first time with her.

"It's a lot like Wolf Valley. A small town, but it's a little bigger than Wolf Valley. We can look around if you'd like," I offer.

"Maybe."

The sun is already starting to set as we drive down the main street, and I decide to do a pass so that she can see all of the shops before I head back towards Pasha, the Mediterranean restaurant.

"I love Greek food!" Mira says as soon as she sees me park outside of the restaurant.

"I know," I say before I can think better of it.

She frowns over at me and I scramble to think of an excuse, but I don't want to lie to her. I'm all in with Mira. Maybe it's about time that she knows that.

"I've seen you looking at a lot of recipes on your phone," I admit, and she blinks.

"Oh."

I climb out of the Jeep and go around to her side to open

her door for her. She smiles at me distractedly, her eyes looking at Pasha and the shops on either side of it.

I place my hand on the small of her back and lead her over to the door and inside. It feels so good to be touching Mira like this, so natural, so I decide to leave my hand there as we head to the hostess and check in.

"Right this way," she says, and we follow her towards a table in the back of the restaurant.

The place is just as nice as it looked in the pictures online. There are plants hanging down and covering the back wall where the bar is. Murals of the ocean and beaches cover the other three walls, and I slow my pace when I see Mira staring wide-eyed at the paintings.

We reach the table, and I pull out Mira's chair for her, then sit down across from her. The hostess hands us our menus and Mira smiles her thanks at her as she heads back up front.

"Have you ever been to Greece?" I ask her, and she laughs like the idea is crazy.

"I wish!"

I file that information away for later, already imagining taking her there.

Maybe for our honeymoon...

"Is that your dream vacation?" I ask, and she nods.

"I'd love to go there, but there's so many places I'd like to see someday."

"Do you like traveling?"

"I don't know. I haven't done much of it."

"Really? Your family didn't go on vacations when you were younger?"

"No."

Her smile falls and her voice turns sharper. I'm guessing

that her family or her childhood are sore subjects for her. Looks like we have that in common.

"Yeah, me either," I tell her.

"Really?" She asks, seeming surprised.

"Really. My family... we're not close. I haven't talked to them since I joined the military."

"I'm not close to mine either. It was just my mom and me growing up. I haven't talked to her since I moved out."

"Hi there, and welcome to Pasha," our waiter says as he stops next to our table.

I hurry to open my menu and scan the list of drinks.

"Can I get you two something to drink and maybe an appetizer?" He asks us.

"I'll just have water," I order.

"Me too," Mira orders.

"Would you like any appetizers?" He asks.

I look at Mira, and she scans the menu.

"What looks good to you?" She asks me, and I shrug.

"Get whatever you want. What do you recommend?" I ask the waiter.

"I love the hummus and pita and the Spanakopita," he tells us.

"That sounds good. Let's try that," Mira says.

"Sounds good."

The waiter nods, writing down our order as he turns to head back to the kitchen. We both glance at our menus, and I decide on the chicken gyro. Mira takes longer to study the menu, biting her lip as she tries to decide what to order.

"What brought you to Wolf Valley?" I ask her when she closes the menu.

"It was cheap," she says with a self-conscious laugh. "I was living in California before, and it was just getting to be too expensive. When I was laid off from my job there, I knew that I needed to make a change."

The waiter comes back with our drinks and appetizers. He pulls out his notepad and we both order. As soon as he's gone, we both dig into the appetizers.

"What about you?" She asks as she takes a bite of Spanakopita.

"Xavier was from here, and I wanted to stay close to him."

"He's your best friend."

"More like a brother at this point," I admit, and she smiles.

"That's nice. I was an only child and it could be lonely."

"Same. I used to wish for a brother or sister. When I got older, I was kind of glad that it was just me. Having a sibling would have tied me to that family more. Unless they were willing to leave too."

"I know. I was the same way," she says.

We finish the appetizers and our food is dropped off a minute later. The conversation turns to lighter subjects, and I learn that she loves salty food over sweets, her favorite color is green, she loves the cold more than the heat, and she's always wanted a house with a fireplace and a dog or two.

All of that information has been filed away, and I'm determined to give her all of those things. We'll live in a green house that's always cold, has at least two fireplaces and a kitchen that is stocked full of salty snacks, and has a whole pack of dogs running around.

"Did you save room for dessert?" The waiter asks as he clears our plates.

"Oh, no," Mira says, rubbing her stomach. "I'm stuffed."

"We'll take the baklava cheesecake to go then," I say, and she smiles at me.

"You got it," the waiter says.

He drops off the check as he heads to grab our dessert, and I pay, shaking my head when Mira tries to give me some money.

"It's my treat."

She looks like she wants to argue, but the waiter is back with our to-go dessert, and I stand, offering her my hand as we get ready to leave.

I lead her back outside and over to my Jeep. I open the door for her and then pass her the dessert.

"Did you want to try to check out any of the shops?" I ask her, and she shakes her head.

"I think a lot of them are closing. Maybe another time," she says, and I smile.

"Planning another date already?" I ask her, and she smirks.

"No, I was going to go by myself," she sasses.

"Liar. We'll come again soon," I promise her.

I close her door, climb behind the wheel, and make the short drive back to Wolf Valley. The streets are nearly deserted as I park outside of Mira's apartment and hop out to walk her upstairs.

Mira seems more relaxed with me as we climb up to her apartment. I'm hoping that's a good sign because I'm about to ask her out on another date, and I desperately want her to say yes.

"Thanks for dinner," she tells me, and I smile.

"Anytime. In fact, why don't we do this again sometime?"

A pink flush covers her cheeks and she smiles up at me.

"Okay, that sounds like fun."

I want to fist bump and cheer, but I'm afraid that would scare her off so I refrain and just grin down at her.

"Tomorrow?"

"I have work. I'm free on Friday, though."

"Friday then."

She smiles up at me, and my heart starts to race as I lean down towards her. She licks her lips and I close the gap between us and press my mouth against hers.

Her lips are soft and firm beneath mine, and she sighs as her head tilts, giving me better access to her mouth. I lick the seam of her lips, and she gasps, opening for me.

She tastes like Greek spices, and I reach up, cupping her face in my hands. Her tongue flicks against mine shyly, and I swear that I nearly come in my pants.

A door slams beneath us, and Mira jumps, pulling back from me. Her eyes are wide and hazy looking as she stares up at me. Her lips are red and swollen from mine, and all that I can think about is kissing her again.

"Night," she whispers, stepping back from me, and I clear my throat.

"Good night, Mira."

I wait while she unlocks the door and heads inside before I turn and jog back outside to my Jeep. I've got another date lined up with my dream girl and my lips are still buzzing from our first kiss.

Things are finally looking up for me.

I smile the whole way home.

FIVE

Mira

I SMILE as I brush out my hair. I've been doing that a lot lately. Ever since my date with Townes the other night. He's been stopping by work the last two days and bringing me food on my breaks. It's kind of been like a little date. I've been living for those stolen moments with him.

I've been learning so much about him. It's kind of crazy how much we have in common. We both didn't have the best childhoods and neither of us talks to our families now.

Tonight, we're going on another real date. He wouldn't tell me what he had planned for us, but I'm sure that I'm going to love it. Townes seems to hang on my every word, and he remembers everything that I so much as mention. He seems to know all of my likes and dislikes already.

I kind of love that he's been paying so much attention to me. He seems to file away everything that I've ever said that I like or dislike. I love being with him. He makes me laugh and smile more than anyone else. I just wish that he wasn't so bossy sometimes.

I'm not even sure if bossy is the right word. He just takes charge of situations and tells me that we're doing something rather than asking. I know that I'm probably just being sensitive and that getting ordered around just reminds me of my mom, but I still can't seem to shake the annoyance everytime he does it.

I finish getting ready and just in time because Townes knocks on my door as I'm tugging my shoes on.

I opted to dress up a bit more tonight and put on the one and only dress that I own and the only pair of high heels as well. The dress fits a little tighter than I remember, but Townes seems to love my curves, and I think that they're shown off nicely in this dress.

The black material hugs my breasts and is snug around my waist and hips. It ends just above my knees and I smooth the material down as I head to answer the door.

"Hey -eh," Townes says as I open the door.

His eyes widen as he takes me in and then he just stares at me, his mouth hanging open slightly. His reaction is a major ego boost for me and I stand straighter, more confidently.

"Hey," I greet him, taking him in.

He's wearing jeans and a flannel shirt. His muscles fill out the shirt and make him look like a lumberjack. A sexy one.

"You look..." he starts, trailing off as his eyes travel down my body again.

"Good?" I supply, and he nods, his eyes locked on my hips, then my legs, and then back up to my face.

"Gorgeous," he says, his voice deep with heat.

"Thanks," I say, and I can feel my cheeks heating with a blush.

I grab my purse and pull my door shut behind me, locking it and dropping my keys into my bag.

"Where are we going tonight?" I ask him, and he takes my hand and helps me down the stairs.

"I thought that I would cook for you tonight. If that sounds good to you?"

"Sounds perfect."

He helps me into his Jeep and I try to contain my excitement at the thought of being alone with Townes. I've never seen his place, and I try to imagine what it looks like. Townes is kind of a grumpy, no-frills guy, so I bet that it's a typical bachelor pad with just a leather couch and a big TV.

He pulls up outside of a cabin that's surprisingly bigger than I expected. It's surrounded by forests, but still looks warm and inviting. He parks and hurries to open my door while I look around.

"Here, careful. There might be some ice there," he says as he takes my hand and helps me out of the car.

We hurry through the cold wind and inside. I freeze as soon as the door closes behind us.

His house is nothing like I expected. There's a leather couch and flatscreen TV, sure, but there's also throw pillows and rugs. There are a few pictures on the mantle of Xavier, Townes, and a few other soldiers.

"Come on, I'll show you around."

I take off my coat, and he tosses it over an armchair as we head down the hallway. He opens the first door, and I peek in, spotting an office.

"This is where I work. Right down here is a bathroom and then the kitchen."

He leads me into a large kitchen that looks like a chef's

dream. There's a fancy looking oven and stone, marble countertops, and dark wood cabinets. Everything is gleaming and looks brand new, and I wonder how much time he spends in the kitchen.

"What are you making for us tonight?" I ask him as he heads over to the shiny fridge.

"I thought that we could have spaghetti."

"Sounds good. Can I help with anything?"

"No, I've got it. Can I get you something to drink?"

"Sure."

"Wine? Water?"

"Wine, please."

He nods and grabs a bottle of white wine.

"Is this alright?"

"I don't know much about wine, but I'm sure it will be good."

He pours us each a glass and I take a sip, savoring the sweet taste. Townes moves around the kitchen, filling a pot with water and turning on the stove. He grabs a box of spaghetti and a jar of sauce. I watch as he pulls a loaf of garlic bread out of the freezer and opens that.

"Do you cook often?" I ask him, and he nods.

"Yeah. I had to learn how to at a young age if I wanted to eat," he tells me, and I nod.

"I wish that I was better at it. My mom, she had a lot of... mental health problems," I hedge. "She didn't like me touching things in our house. If I did, we'd have to wash them three times."

"Why three times?" He asks with a frown, and I shrug.

"She has undiagnosed OCD. She did a lot of things three times. She was also a huge germaphobe and was terrified of the outside world. I had to go to school and then straight home. When I got home, I'd shower and change my clothes. Then we'd clean."

"Sounds hard," he says softly, and I nod.

"It was. It was stifling and so restrictive."

"I'm sorry, Mira."

"I tried to get her help," I tell him, and he looks at me with sad eyes. "But she didn't want it. Said that there was nothing wrong with her."

"Maybe she'll realize she's wrong one day," he offers, and I give him a sad smile.

"I doubt it."

We're silent for a moment as the water starts to boil behind him.

"My parents were drug addicts. I tried to get them help too, but it never worked. In order to get better, they'd have to want that, and they never did."

"I'm so sorry, Townes."

He nods, opening the box of spaghetti and fiddling with the cardboard.

"I can't fix them, and the sad truth is that I'm better off without them. Happier."

"Good."

He smiles slightly, and I smile back.

"I'm happier without her too."

We share a smile, and he goes back to cooking.

"I like your house," I tell him, and he grins over his shoulder at me.

"Thanks. I need to finish the tour later."

"After dinner," I say, and he nods.

I watch him move around the kitchen, and I can feel my core clenching as he stirs the spaghetti and bends to grab a baking tray for the garlic bread. There's something so sexy about seeing him cook for me.

I take another sip of wine before I stand and move to his side.

"Here, let me help with that," I say, grabbing the jar of spaghetti sauce.

"No, I've got it," he says, trying to take the jar back from me.

The only problem is that I had already opened the lid, and when he grabs it, I end up holding the lid as the spaghetti sauce spills all over my dress, shoes, and the floor between us.

"Shit, Mira! I'm so sorry," Townes apologizes as he sets the jar aside and reaches for some paper towels.

"It was an accident," I say, taking the paper towels and trying to wipe up the sauce.

"That's going to stain. Let me wash it for you. You can take a shower and borrow some of my clothes," he tells me.

"That would be good, thanks."

I follow him upstairs and down the hallway to his room. As soon as I step inside, I freeze.

"Are you painting in here?" I ask him as I spot the half-finished walls.

"Oh, yeah. I just... thought that it needed a change."

I stare at the freshly painted green walls and try not to read too much into it.

He leads me into the bathroom and sets clean towels on the vanity.

"I'll throw your clothes in the wash once you're done. Just let me know if you need anything," he says, and I nod.

"Sure, thanks."

He nods and leaves the bathroom and I take a deep breath, step out of my shoes and pull off my dress. I try to rinse off the sauce in the sink and then leave the dress to dry on the counter.

I turn the shower on and try not to think about the fact that I'm about to be naked in Townes' house.

The water pressure is amazing, and I moan as I let the warm water wash over me. I grab his body wash and scrub off the spaghetti sauce from my legs and feet. I rub the soap over my breasts and bite my lip as a wave of lust slams into me at his scent on me.

I shut the water off, trying to get my libido under control as I wrap a towel around my body. I dry off, but as the cotton rubs against my heated skin, I find myself having a naughty thought.

I could walk out to Townes in just his towel. I wonder what he would do? Would he make a move on me? Do I want him to?

Yes.

The answer is there so fast and I feel alive for the first time in my life. I want him.

I roll my shoulders back and take a deep, steadying breath as I walk out of the bathroom in just a towel.

I'm heading towards the door when it opens, and Townes freezes in the doorway, his eyes locked on me.

He clears his throat, tearing his eyes away from my still-damp legs to look me in the eyes.

"Sorry, I just realized that I never set out clothes for you," he says, and I smile.

"That's okay. I don't mind."

I take a step toward him, trying to show him that I want him, and I smile when I see Townes swallow hard, his eyes dropping back to my towel-covered curves.

My heart races and an awareness skitters along my skin. I can feel it.

Something big is about to happen.

SIX

Townes

I'VE HAD dreams like this a lot since I first met Mira.

Maybe that's why I don't react right away as she walks towards me, dripping wet and wearing only my towel. It isn't until she reaches out, her fingers brushing against my arm tentatively, that I snap out of my daze and realize this isn't a dream.

This is really happening.

Fucking finally.

I reach for her, pulling her into my arms and flush against my body. She lets out a little gasp and I smile as I cup her jaw and tilt her face up towards mine. Her green eyes meet mine and then flutter shut as I dip my head and claim her lips with mine.

Her lips and skin are still damp from her shower, and her hair drips water onto my arms as I pull her closer to me. All I can think about is if she's this wet for me between her thighs.

Her lips are soft but firm against mine, and I slip my hands into her hair, holding her in place as our lips meet over and over again. I feel like I'm in a daze or maybe a dream when she finally pulls away.

"You're too tall," she says with a laugh as she drops back down onto her feet.

I hadn't even realized that I had pulled her up onto her tiptoes when I was kissing her. I wrap my arm tighter around her waist and lift her up off the ground.

She gasps, her arms wrapping around me as she clings to me.

"Now wrap your legs around my waist," I order, and she blushes.

"Then the towel will come undone," she whispers, and I give her a wicked grin.

"Uh-huh, and I'll be able to see all of those sexy curves. Isn't that what you wanted? I know damn sure that it's what I want."

Her cheeks flush, but she does as I say and wraps her thick thighs around my waist. She presses fully against me, and I nearly come just from feeling all of her curves pressed against me.

Sure enough, the towel knot loosens and comes undone, falling to the ground.

I hold her eyes for a beat, and it feels like neither of us is breathing. Then my eyes dip down, and I groan at what I see.

I suddenly regret holding her because it means that I can't touch her the way that I want to.

"I'm going to need to get those tits in my mouth," I tell her as I start walking toward my bed.

Mira's grip on me tightens, and I smirk as I realize that she likes my dirty mouth.

I lay her down, and in the next instant, I'm cupping the soft mounds of her breasts in my hands. They fit perfectly, and I roll the stiff peaks of her nipples between my thumbs and forefingers until she gasps and arches into my touch.

"That feels so-oh good," she gasps, and I grin.

"We're just getting started."

My head dips and I lick one nipple and then the other, alternating until I hear her breathing pick up. She's panting, her body restless beneath me, and I know that I'm driving us both crazy.

I give her a kiss right between her tits and drop to my knees at the edge of the bed. Her eyes are half-lidded as I grab her thighs, but they fly open as I tug her to the edge of the bed.

"Townes!" She cries, and I give her a devilish smirk as I wrap my hands around her thighs and bury my face between her legs.

"Oh!" She screams at the first lick.

I moan, her sweet flavor exploding over my taste buds. Just like that, I'm instantly addicted.

I bury my face deeper in her soft folds and eat her like a starving man. My tongue licks over her clit, and her thighs spasm around my head. When I do it again, her legs clamp down around my head. When I do it a third time, she comes against my mouth.

"Townes!" She screams, and my cock demands attention behind the zipper of my jeans.

"Fuck, I love hearing you scream my name like that," I tell her, my thumb moving to her core.

I find her clit and start to rub lazy circles over the sensitive pearl.

"Please," she begs, and I smile.

"I've got you," I promise her.

I push a finger inside of her, surprised at just how tight she is.

Could she be...?

"Are you a virgin?" I blurt out, and her blushing cheeks give me my answer.

"Um, yes," she says softly.

"Shit, Mira. Are we going too fast?" I ask, already pulling away from her.

"No! Don't stop. I want this."

I study her for a moment, but she seems sincere. My heart jumps in my chest as I realize that she must like me as much as I do her. She wouldn't be giving me this honor otherwise.

"I have no idea what I did to deserve you, but I swear that I'll never stop doing it."

She smiles slightly, and I push a finger back inside of her, determined to loosen her up some before I try to make love to her.

Her hips start to move as I slowly slide my finger in and out of her snug channel. Soon, I'm adding a second finger and then a third. It only takes a few pumps before she's coming again, and I can't take it anymore.

I kiss her clit and then stand and start tearing at my clothes. She watches me with half-lidded eyes until I strip off my jeans and boxers. Then her eyes widen and lock on my hard-on.

"I'll go slow," I promise, and she nods.

I climb onto the bed next to her and then move us both to the middle of the mattress.

Her hands cling to my biceps, and I know that I need to help her relax, so I lean forward and cup her face with one hand, pulling her mouth towards mine. Our lips meet, and she opens for me right away, letting me slip my tongue into her mouth. I wonder if she can taste herself on my lips.

Her tongue flicks against the tip of mine, and I growl, my hand sliding around to the back of her head, and I hold her in place as our tongues battle together.

"Townes," she moans against my lips, and my fingers tighten in her hair.

Her hands move cautiously down my chest and stomach. I grab them before she can wrap her fingers around my cock.

She blinks, frowning at me as I grit my teeth.

"Don't you want me to..." she asks, trailing off.

"God, yes. Right now, though, I need to be inside you. You can explore me later," I promise her.

She nods, and I move her under me. Her thighs spread in invitation, and I have to remind myself that this isn't a dream as I line my cock up with her tight opening.

Our eyes meet as I push in an inch, and she lets out a shaky breath.

"Good?" I ask her, praying that it is.

"Uh huh," she moans, her hips shifting under me, pushing me in a little more.

Her green eyes are dark now and filled with lust as she watches me. I push in another inch and bump up against her virginity.

"Fuck," I hiss.

She's moaning beneath me, which has to be a good sign, but I'm hanging on by a thread here and hearing her moan for me, feeling her tits rubbing against my chest; it's all too much. I'm going to come before I can even fuck her properly.

Make this good for her! I scold myself, and I grit my teeth as I thrust forward and pop her cherry.

She inhales sharply as I fill her fully, and I study her, praying that I didn't hurt her. She blinks up at me, her mouth falling open.

"I'm so... full," she gasps as I start to move tentatively inside of her.

"Is it too much?" I ask her.

Please say no, please say no, please say no.

"No, it feels good," she says.

Thank God.

I start to move more then, pulling almost all of the way out before I slide back in. I do that over and over again, letting her get used to the size and feel of me. Soon, she's rocking her hips in sync with my thrusts.

Having my dream girl beneath me is the hottest thing that I've ever seen in my life. Hearing her soft sighs and moans is driving me wild, and I know that I won't be able to last much longer.

I lean back on my heels so that I can rub her clit. The change in angle has her eyes lighting up, and I start to fuck her harder as my own orgasm starts to brew inside of me.

"Townes! Oh-ohh God!" She cries as her pussy clamps down around me.

I grit my teeth, determined to get her off before I come.

I press more firmly on her clit as I pound into her, and she screams my name as she comes. Feeling her juices coat my cock has me following her over the edge, and I choke out her name as I come with her.

"Oh," she whispers as we both catch our breaths, and I laugh as I collapse on the mattress next to her.

"Oh?" I ask her, and she giggles.

"Yeah, oh."

"Hmm, you're hurting my ego here. I think I'm going to

need a redo so I can try for a better reaction than oh," I tell her, and she gives me a little smirk.

"Well, I *guess* that you can have one more chance," she says, and I grin as I pull her against me.

"Challenge accepted," I whisper a second before my lips land on hers.

SEVEN

Mira

WHEN I FIRST OPEN MY eyes, I'm so confused. This isn't my apartment, and why am I so warm? Then I feel Townes' arms tighten around me and last night comes rushing back to me.

He had made love to me twice before we finally left bed and went downstairs to eat. It was midnight by the time the spaghetti was ready, and we had laughed and talked while we ate, then headed right back up to bed to make love again.

I must have passed out after that. It's bright outside, and I wonder what time it is as I try to wiggle my way out from beneath Townes' arms.

"Where are you going?" He mumbles sleepily, and I look over my shoulder to see his eyes still closed.

"To the bathroom," I whisper, and he grumbles but lets me go.

I scoot off the bed and head into the bathroom. It feels so strange to walk around naked like this. My body is sore, and I notice a few bruises and red marks from his hands and mouth on my hips and breasts.

I go to the bathroom and study my reflection as I wash my hands. I guess I thought that I would feel different after I had lost my virginity, but I still feel like me. I run my fingers through my brown hair, trying to untangle some of the knots.

I head back to the bedroom where Townes is sitting in bed. He smiles when he sees me and crooks a finger at me, silently telling me to come back to bed.

"I need to get home," I tell him as I head back towards him.

"It's still early," he argues.

"It's almost nine," I say with a laugh.

He glares at the alarm clock on his bedside table, and I wrap my arms around his neck.

"I really do need to go. I have a long to-do list today."

"Alright. Will I see you tonight? I can make us dinner again."

"Maybe. Let me see how today goes."

He looks like he wants to argue with me, to demand an answer right here and now, but he bites his tongue and leans forward and kisses me instead.

I pull back before he can deepen it, and he growls, trying to pull me back towards him.

"The faster I leave and get everything done, the faster I can come back," I remind him, and he sighs but lets me go.

"Fine. Go do what you have to. Or better yet, you could let me come and help," he offers.

"Don't you have work?"

"Probably," he admits, and I laugh.

"Go do that. I'll see you later."

I grab the dress from last night that we never managed to wash off his dresser, but he stops me.

"You can borrow something from me."

"It's fine. I'm just going home, and then I'll change there."

"Here," he says like I didn't say anything. "You can wear this."

He passes me a shirt and sweatpants, and part of me wants to argue with him, but what does it matter in the end?

"Thanks," I mumble as I get dressed and follow him downstairs.

"Just going to your apartment?" He asks me as we head outside to his Jeep. "Or do you want to stop for breakfast?"

"No, just my apartment."

"Are you sure? You have to eat," he says, and annoyance prickles at my skin.

"I'm sure."

He starts the Jeep and we head towards my apartment in silence. His words stick with me, and it isn't until he's dropped me off and I'm standing in my apartment that it hits me why.

He's bossing me around just like my mom used to. He acts like he knows better than me, like what he wants is more important.

I look down at the clothes that I didn't even want to borrow and frown. Was I warmer in them? Yes, but I had said that I didn't need to wear his stuff. Then, I just let him bulldoze me.

I'm mad at myself for not standing up to him, but I'm also mad at Townes for bossing me around.

My phone buzzes and I pull it out, scowling when I see that it's from Townes.

. . .

TOWNES: I'm at Nosh. I'll pick you up something to eat and drop it off in a bit.

Mira: That's okay. I have stuff here.

Townes: It's no problem. See you soon.

I WANT TO SCREAM, but I settle for gritting my teeth and tossing my phone onto the counter. I pace back and forth around my small living room.

It's been almost two years since I left my mom's house, and I'm sure that the anniversary is bringing up old feelings too, but I can't shake the annoyance and anger I'm feeling about Townes's behavior.

I head into my room to shower and get changed, hoping that helps calm me down. It does. For a bit.

"Hey, breakfast is here," Townes says as I'm drying my hair.

I scream, ducking away from him in shock.

"Shit! You scared the crap out of me," I tell him, my hand covering my racing heart.

"You shouldn't leave your door unlocked," he tells me, and I grind my teeth together.

"Got it. Thanks for breakfast."

"Anytime."

He leans forward, kisses me, and then smiles as he turns and heads out of my apartment. I wait until he's gone before I grab the nearest pillow and scream into it.

This is all too much too fast. I mean, I was just starting to really stand on my own two feet, and now it feels like I'm suffocating. I know I'm probably just overwhelmed, but I can't shake the feeling that maybe jumping into a relationship right now isn't the best idea.

I mean, I was trying to find my freedom and myself, and

instead, it feels like I just tied myself down with a grumpy, bossy man.

Did I mess up? Did I just trade one overbearing dictator for another?

Townes cares about me, and I know that he isn't my mother, but it's hard not to make the comparison or to wonder.

I lock my front door and drag my hands down my face as I wonder what the heck I should do now.

EIGHT

Townes

"GOING TO SEE YOUR GIRL?" Ford asks as he bags up my to go order.

"Yeah, I'm bringing her dinner."

He nods, his eyes sliding over to where Cameron, one of the waitresses who works for him, is talking to a customer.

"I'm happy for you," he says quietly, and I smile.

"Thanks. When are you going to make your move?" I ask, nodding in Cameron's direction.

"Soon," he says, and there's a determined light in his eyes.

I know that feeling. Watching Xavier fall in love with Olive and seeing how happy they are now made me want that with Mira all the more. I'm sure that it's the same for Ford. He's had to watch his twin brother, Foster, finally get his girl, and now his closest friends are all settling down too. I'm glad that he's finally going to go for it with Cameron.

Ford passes me the bag of food, and I wave as I grab it

and head out to my Jeep. Mira is working at Wet and Wild tonight, but we've been eating in my Jeep behind the building to try to stay warm. Plus, it gives us enough privacy to make out a little bit.

I park in our usual spot and leave the Jeep running so that it's warm when Mira comes out. I grab my phone and send Mira a text to let her know that I'm outside, and then I wait for my girl.

These moments with her are the brightest spots in my day. I wake up looking forward to seeing her later. I spend all day counting down the hours until I can see her again.

The back door opens, and I sit up straighter, greedy for my first sight of her. She's wearing jeans and the black Wet and Wild work shirt and pulling on her jacket as she heads over toward my Jeep.

I hop out and smile as she looks at me. She smiles back, but it's not as bright as usual, and I pause as I reach to open the passenger door for her.

"How's work going?" I ask her, wondering if something happened tonight.

"Pretty good. We had two bachelorette parties come in, so it's been busy."

"That's good. I got you a burger and fries from Nosh," I say, and she smiles weakly.

I close the door, hurry over to the driver's side, and climb in next to her. She's opening the take-out bag and hands me the first container before she pulls out the second.

"Thanks for dinner," she says, and even her voice is subdued tonight.

"Is everything okay?" I ask her, starting to get worried.

"Yeah, I'm just tired. It's been a long day," she says.

She does look a little tired and I try to let the nagging feeling go as we both dig into our burgers and fries.

She finishes her food quickly and leans back in her seat, letting her head rest against the seat as she closes her eyes. I toss our trash back in the bag and turn to face her more.

"Are you working tomorrow?" I ask her, and she shakes her head.

"No, I have tomorrow and the next day off."

"Are we just going to be hanging out at home then? I can go to the store tonight and grab some snacks and food so we don't have to leave the house at all."

"That sounds amazing... but I need to get some things done around my apartment tomorrow."

"Tomorrow night then," I try, and she chews on her bottom lip and looks out the window.

"Maybe. I'll let you know."

My stomach cramps, and I realize that she's pulling back from me.

I try not to panic. After all, she could really need to do stuff at her apartment, or maybe she just wants to sleep in her own bed and decompress.

"Sure," I say, and I can hear the disappointment in my voice.

"I should get back in there. Thanks again for dinner."

"Anytime."

She reaches for her door handle and I frown and stop her.

"I'll get your door," I tell her, and she sighs, seeming frustrated as she sits back and waits for me.

I hurry to get out and get her door for her. She hops out and avoids my eyes as she brushes past me.

"I'll talk to you later?" I ask, and she nods.

"Yeah," she says softly, and I want to reach out and grab her.

I want to make her face me, to demand that she tell me

what's wrong so I can fix it. I know that would only make her close up more though so I squeeze my fingers into my palms and stand still.

"Night, Townes," she says before she heads inside, and I swallow, trying to dislodge the rock in my throat.

"Good night, Mira."

The door closes behind her, and I stand there in the cold for another minute, praying that she'll come back out and tell me that this was all some kind of terrible joke.

She doesn't though, and I shiver as the wind blows my hair across my forehead. I hurry back to the driver's side and shift into drive.

I head towards Xavier's house, but when I pull up outside, his truck is gone, and I know he must be out with Olive. I turn around and head back towards town, trying to figure out where to go now.

I wind up at the Wolf Valley Market and decide to get groceries on the off chance that Mira comes over to stay this weekend.

I park and head inside, grabbing a cart and wandering aimlessly up and down each aisle. I spot a familiar head of brown hair in the cereal aisle and smile as I head over to Ransom.

"Hey," I greet him, and he looks up, giving me a lazy smile.

"Hey, are you getting groceries for the week too?" He asks, looking at my mostly empty cart.

"More like the weekend, but I don't know what I want to eat really."

"Cereal is always a safe choice," he says, tossing two boxes of Cinnamon Toast Crunch into the cart.

"True," I say, grabbing a box for myself too.

"I'm surprised that you're here. I figured that you would

be out with your girlfriend," he says as we turn and head down the aisle.

"She has to work tonight."

"Hmm," he says, eyeing a box of oatmeal for a moment before he passes. "What are you doing for Valentine's Day?"

"Valentine's Day?" I ask in confusion, and he snorts.

"Yeah, you know, that holiday for people in love? They have it every year in February. This isn't ringing any bells?" He asks with a smirk, and I glare at him.

"It is... I just forgot. I've never celebrated it before," I tell him.

"Me either," he says with a shrug. "Though I might try to this year."

"Ah, with Ruby," I say, and he frowns.

"Am I really that obvious about it?" He grumbles more to himself, and I shrug.

"I should make reservations somewhere," I say, and he nods.

"Or plan some kind of romantic night in. What are you going to do for presents?" He asks me as we turn and head down the chip aisle.

"Candy and flowers, I guess. It seems like I should keep it classic."

"Sounds like a plan."

He tosses in a few bags of chips, and I grab some pretzels and popcorn since I know that Mira loves them.

We brainstorm other ideas for Valentine's Day as we finish shopping and head to checkout.

"I'll see you later," he says as we head out to our cars.

"See you."

We head in opposite directions, and I hurry to load all

of the groceries into my Jeep and push the cart back up to the market.

I drive by Wet and Wild on my way home and crane my neck to try to get a glimpse of Mira, but she must be in one of the aisles or in the back. I head home and unpack all of the groceries. Then I just stand in my kitchen.

Something feels off with Mira, but I can't figure out what could have caused that. We had fun on our last date. She's been normal when I bring her food at work. We've been texting like usual. Nothing seems off. Until tonight.

I try to convince myself that it's all in my head, but as I clean up the kitchen and get ready for bed, all I can think about is how I'm messing things up with Mira.

I pull out my phone and plug it into the charger next to my bed. There's no message from Mira, but she's probably just getting home. I decide to text her and click on her name.

TOWNES: Good night. I'll talk to you tomorrow. Sweet dreams.

I STARE AT THE SCREEN, waiting for the dots to pop up so that I know she's texting me back, but they never come.

I frown at the screen. She's usually so quick to text me back, and panic starts to set in once again.

I lay back in bed and stare at the ceiling. All I can think is that I'm not going to lose Mira. Not when I finally have her.

Sleep doesn't come for a very long time.

NINE

Mira

I'M LOST.

Not literally. I mean, I'm standing in the middle of Shelf Indulgence. No, I'm lost with what to do.

It's been three days since I last talked to Townes. I thought that time and space away from him would help me clear my head and figure out what to do. Instead, it's left me feeling even more torn.

It's been hard to ignore him. I've been avoiding his calls and texts, refusing to answer when he knocked on my apartment door yesterday. I know that my time is running out though. He knows I'm working today, so it's only a matter of time before he shows up here.

I clock in and force a smile to my lips as I greet Saffron and head over to the front counter to see what I need to stock today.

"Mira," Townes says behind me, and I jump, spinning to face him.

That was fast.

"Hey," I say awkwardly.

Looking at him hurts. He looks so worried and confused. I hate that I did this to him. I never wanted to hurt him, and now I'm afraid that I'm going to hurt us both.

"Can we talk?" He asks me, and I look around, hoping Saffron will save me.

"Go ahead, Mira! We're slow right now," she says with a smile.

I'm sure she thinks she's being helpful, so I smile back at her and then lead Townes over to a deserted corner of the store.

"What's up?" I ask, trying to sound nonchalant.

"What's up? You tell me?" He growls. "Why are you ignoring me? You haven't answered any of my texts or calls. I came by your place yesterday, and I know you were home."

"I must have been sleeping," I lie, and he narrows his eyes at me.

"You're lying."

I swallow hard, crossing my arms over my chest and looking away from him.

"What happened, Mira? I thought things were good between us, and then you started to ice me out. What did I do?"

His words break my heart, and I clear my throat, trying to remove the lump forming there.

"Nothing. You didn't do anything. It's me. Things are just moving really fast between us, and I'm not sure I'm ready for that."

"Fine, then say that. We can slow down."

"Can we? Ever since we started dating, you've seemed to have one speed. I mean, we've only been together for like a week and a half, and we spend all of our free time together."

"I like spending time with you," he says, sounding confused and hurt.

"I do, too, I just... I don't even know," I admit.

Tears burn the backs of my eyes and I try to blink them back.

"I'm scared, Townes," I whisper, and he tries to pull me into his arms, but I push him away.

"You've experienced so much. You've seen the world. I've seen a few towns in the surrounding two hundred miles."

"So, we'll travel more."

"It's not just that. It's me," I stress, the first tears falling onto my cheeks.

"Mira..."

"I don't think you realize how isolated and alone I was growing up. It was just my mom and me. No friends, no boyfriends, nothing. Then I came here and I made friends. I have two jobs that I love, my own apartment, and my own space. I'm in charge of my life and I love that freedom. I'm trying to figure out what I like and it was going well."

I stop, but I can see that he knows where I'm going.

"Until you met me," he says quietly, and I choke back a sob.

"Not just that. I like you. A lot. I just feel like I'm losing myself. I'm so scared to go back to where it's just me and one person. I want to have friends and a life, and I think I would give that all away for you already."

"I would never ask you to do that," he insists, and I swipe at the tears.

"Maybe not on purpose, but you have a habit of taking over or bulldozing me."

"How?"

"Insisting on me not helping you cook, demanding that you open my door for me," I list off.

"I was just trying to be a gentleman," he says, and I nod.

"I know, but it triggers me. It reminds me of my mom bossing me around. I don't mind you doing that stuff sometimes, but I want to be independent. It's important to me."

"Okay, I can back off."

I sigh. *He says that but what happens if he can't? Can I trust him to keep his word? What do I want to do here?*

"I just... I need space."

"Mira, please don't do this," he begs, and I squeeze my lips together, trying to fight off the fresh wave of tears.

"I have to."

"No, you don't. Don't do this. Please. I love you, Mira. I have since I first saw you. I can't lose you," he says, tears sparkling in his eyes.

His words and seeing him like this breaks me, and I sob, tears spilling onto my cheeks.

"I need time," I choke out before I brush past him and run into the back room.

The door closes behind me, and I lean back against the wall and cry.

"Mira? Are you okay?" Saffron asks gently, and I shake my head.

"No," I sob. "I'm pretty sure I just broke my heart and Townes'," I admit.

Her arms wrap around me, and I lean into her hold, letting her try to keep me together as my heart breaks more in my chest.

I don't even remember going home and I know that Saffron must have taken me and made sure that I made it back to my apartment alright. I must have fallen asleep at some point and I wake up to my phone buzzing on the nightstand next to me.

It's still dark out and my first thought is that it's Townes calling me. When I look at the screen though, I'm shocked to see my mom's name there instead.

I stare at it, debating what to do.

Why is she calling me? What could she possibly want? Could she be reaching out because she changed and wants to apologize?

I chew on my bottom lip, debating what to do for so long that the call goes to voicemail. My phone dings with an alert that I have a new voicemail, and I collapse back onto my mattress.

I'm still so raw after breaking up with Townes, and I just can't deal with my mom right now on top of all of that. I'll call her back later.

I close my eyes and try to go back to sleep, but I can't. My mind is racing, and with a sigh, I open my eyes and stare up at the ceiling until the sun starts to spread light around the room.

Finally, I feel strong enough to listen to her message and I grab my phone.

I don't realize that I've gotten my hopes up until I press play, and my mom's nasally voice screeches at me.

"Mira, you need to call me back. I need you to come home and help me. The landlord is raising the rent, and I'm not moving, so you need to come home and help with the bills. It's time for you to start being a good daughter and help your poor mother for once in your life. Call me back so that I know when to expect you."

The message ends, and I let out a deep breath as tears start to spill onto my cheeks.

She wants me to come home. To fix things for her. To help her, even though she's never done anything to help me.

She doesn't even miss me. She just needs me to make her life easier, and she's going to manipulate and boss me around until she gets what she wants.

I can't help but compare Townes and his version of ordering me around with my mom. Townes can be bossy, but he's always looking out for me, and I know that he has my best interests at heart, even if his highhandedness can be a bit annoying at times.

Was it unfair to lump the two of them together? Did I just mess up the best thing to ever happen to me?

I curl up in bed and debate that until the sun starts to set and my eyes are too tired to keep open.

TEN

Townes

SO, this is what it feels like to have a broken heart.

It fucking sucks.

It's even worse because everywhere I look, I see Valentine's Day decorations, and it only reminds me that all of the plans I had made for Mira and me this year won't be happening.

I'll be spending the holiday alone.

Again.

I've been trying to give Mira the space she asked for, but I swear to God, it's killing me. The first few days, I tried to pretend like everything was normal. I went into town and had breakfast at the diner with Xavier and my friends. Then Mira came in, and it felt like I got kicked in the stomach.

I drove to the market and saw her walking to work and almost crashed my car. The ache in my chest took hours to fade after that so I just stopped leaving my house. It seemed safer that way.

It hasn't been easier though. I can still smell Mira on my sheets, and I haven't had the heart to wash them yet.

Today is Valentine's Day, and I don't know what to do with myself. The flowers and chocolates I got for Mira are sitting on my kitchen counter. The reservations that I made at the steakhouse in Rosewood have been canceled.

I can't even go out with Xavier to distract myself because he's spending tonight with Olive.

I'm not sure how much more of this I can take. I can feel myself splintering with each passing day. It's a slow death, and I hate it.

I'm a fighter. It's what got me out of my parents' house and away from them. It's why I joined the Army and then became a Ranger. It might not be what Mira wants right now, but I can't just sit around waiting for her. I'm going to fight for her. At least one more time.

I grab my keys, flowers, and chocolates and march out the door. I know that she had tonight off of work, so I head towards her apartment. The lights are on when I park, and I take a deep breath, jog over to the door, and hit the buzzer for her place.

She buzzes me in right away, and I take the stairs two at a time up to her door.

"It was like fifteen dollars, right?" She asks, counting the cash in her hand.

"What?" I ask her, and her head snaps up.

Her eyes meet mine and I take her in. She looks sad and I wonder if maybe she's been missing me.

"Townes... I wasn't; I thought that you were the pizza delivery."

"Oh."

We stare at each other for a moment, and I thrust the flowers and chocolates at her.

"Happy Valentine's Day," I tell her, and she blinks, taking the gifts slowly.

"Oh," she says as her phone starts to buzz on the counter behind her. "Sorry, I should get that."

She turns and grabs her phone, answering it without looking at the screen.

"Hello?" She says, and I can tell that something is wrong from the way that she tenses.

Her back is ramrod straight, and her fingers clench around the bouquet of flowers and box of chocolates.

"I know, Mom. I got your message. I've just been busy. I was going to call you back though and –"

It's her mom?

I thought that they didn't talk. What could she possibly want now? Is that why Mira pushed me away? Did something happen?

I take a step towards her, and she turns, staring blankly at the wall next to me. Tears are starting to form in her eyes, and I can't stand the sight of them.

"Mom, I can't," she chokes out as the first tears fall onto her face.

That's my breaking point, and I step towards her, grabbing the phone and bringing it to my ear.

"She'll call you back if she wants to talk to you," I tell her mom firmly.

She starts to protest loudly, but I hang up and stare down at my girl.

As soon as I end the call, panic sets in. Did I just overstep? Is she going to be pissed at me?

"I'm sorry," I blurt, and she blinks, wiping at the tears.

"Are you?"

I hesitate, and she huffs out a laugh.

"Not really," I admit, deciding to go with honesty. "I fucking hate seeing you upset."

She nods, and I study her, trying to decide how she feels about me being here, but I can't quite read the expression on her face.

"Why are you here?" She asks, and I take a deep breath and launch into my prepared speech.

"I know that you asked for space and time," I start, and her eyes meet mine. "I tried to stay away, but fuck, Mira. It hurts."

Her eyes start to get shiny with more tears, and I hurry on.

"I love you, Mira. I can't be away from you. I need you in my life… so I promise to be whatever you want me to be. I'll never open a door or boss you around. I'll let you be independent. We'll travel anywhere that you want. We'll go at your pace. I'll do whatever you want, be whatever you want. I just need you."

A tear spills onto her cheek, and I hold my breath, waiting to see what she says. It feels like the silence stretches for hours, but I know that it's probably only a few seconds before she breaks it.

"I thought that you were like my mom," she admits, and the breath leaves my lungs in a whoosh.

"I don't mean to be," I rush to tell her, and she shakes her head.

"You're not. Not really. You can be bossy with me, but you do it from a place of love. You want what's best for me."

"I do," I promise her.

"My mom has called me a few times the last few days," she admits. "That was the first time that I've answered, but she's left a couple of messages and each one is her demanding that I do something for her. She doesn't care about me or what I want or need. All she can think about is herself and her own needs and wants."

I want to pull her into my arms and tell her how much I love her, but I can see that she needs to say her peace so I remain silent and still.

"I still want to have more independence, but...I missed you," she says softly, and my knees almost give out in relief.

I brace my hand on the doorframe, and she smiles shyly at me.

"I missed you too. So much," I tell her.

"I trust you. I know that you'll work to give me what I want, what I need," she says, and I nod.

"I would do anything for you," I tell her, and she smiles softly.

She takes a step toward me, and I can't hold back any longer. I cup her face in my hands and kiss her. All of the emotions that I've felt over the last couple of days are poured into the kiss. The pain and longing, the need and love, it's all there.

She gasps, and I slip my tongue into her mouth to tease hers. She tastes like chocolate and whipped cream, and I know that she must be drinking hot chocolate.

The wrapper on the flowers crunches as I step closer to her, and I pause, taking the flowers and chocolates from her and setting them on the table by the front door. Then I grab her and drag her body against mine.

"Townes," she sighs as my lips claim hers once again, and I moan.

"I love you, Mira," I whisper against her mouth.

"I love you too."

My heart feels like it's going to burst in my chest. This is the best moment of my life.

"Sorry to interrupt," comes a voice behind me, and I growl as I break the kiss and turn around.

An amused looking teen is there holding a pizza box, and I grab my wallet, hand him two twenties and grab the pizza from him.

"Have a good night," he says cheerfully.

I turn back to Mira, passing her the pizza, and she tries to hide her grin behind her hand.

"Are you hungry?" She asks, and I nod.

We head inside, and I kick the door closed behind us. She grabs the flowers and chocolates and sets everything down in the kitchen.

"Happy Valentine's Day," I tell her as she opens the chocolates and pops one in her mouth.

"Thank you."

She chews, and I grab two plates from the cabinet and set them next to the pizza.

"Listen, I want to be with you, but I think we still need to talk."

"Okay," I agree, and we take a seat at the counter.

"I like when you take care of me or show that you are thinking of me, but I want to take care of myself too. I want space to grow and explore."

"Whatever you want, Mira. I'll give it to you."

"What about you?" She asks, and I shake my head.

"I just want you to be safe, healthy, and happy. As long as you are, then I'm good."

She smiles at me as she grabs a slice of pizza, and I smile back as I grab my own slice.

This isn't what I envisioned for our Valentine's Day, but as long as I'm with Mira, I'm happy.

"I didn't get you a gift," she tells me as we're cleaning up, and I shrug.

"That's fine. I don't need anything," I assure her.

"I think that I have something else in mind," she says, her voice going low and husky, and my dick stands at attention.

When she runs her hand low over my back, I turn and follow her back towards her bedroom.

ELEVEN

Mira

I DIDN'T QUITE REALIZE how much I missed being with Townes like this until he's pulling my clothes off. Our skin brushes against each other, and I sigh, enjoying the feel of his hot, hard body against mine.

Our clothes are in a pile at our feet, and I smile as he lifts me in his arms easily and carries me over to the bed.

"I missed you so much," he tells me, and I nod.

"I missed you too."

"Now tell me that you love me," he says, then catches himself. "Shit, I'm sorry, Mira. I swear that I'm trying."

"No, it's alright. I kind of like when you're in charge when we're in the bedroom," I admit and he smirks down at me.

"Good," he whispers against the shell of my ear. "Now say it."

"I love you."

His body seems to sag in relief at my words and a thrill

goes through me as I realize the power that I have over him. Townes might like taking control, but he would do anything I asked of him if it made me happy.

That's the difference between my mother and him. My mom couldn't get past her OCD and what she wanted. I needed friends and to have a normal childhood where I wasn't afraid all of the time. She never was willing to work to give me that.

Townes kisses my neck and thoughts of my mother and the past disappear as I get lost in him. He lays me down in the center of my twin-size bed and grumbles a bit as he tries to get comfortable on it next to me.

"Please let me buy you a bigger bed," he begs. "Or better yet, you can just move in with me."

"I like my bed."

He sighs, then moves so that he's above me, caging me in with his arms. My core clenches as I feel his weight on me, and I wrap my arms around his neck, pulling him down until his lips meet mine.

His mouth moves against mine in a slow, decadent kiss. I get lost in him, my hands running over his body everywhere I can reach. I run my hands down his sides, then up his back, over his chest and arms. I can feel his cock harden further between my legs, and I start to grow restless beneath him, my hips lifting so that his length rubs him right where I need him most.

I wrap my legs around his waist, and he laughs against my skin.

"So eager. I need to get you ready for me," he tells me as I continue to rub against him.

"Oh, trust me, I'm more than ready," I assure him.

His dick rubs through my folds, and we both groan at the contact. I arch against him, and he kisses down to my breasts, taking one nipple into his mouth to tease between his teeth.

"Townes," I moan, and he bites down softly on the sensitive nub.

He switches to my other breast, giving it the same attention, and I let my eyes close as we move together.

We're teasing each other, driving both of us closer and closer to the edge. I'm so close to coming and he's not even inside of me yet.

"Please," I beg, and he growls against the swell of my breast.

"Fuck, Mira. You drive me crazy," he groans as he sits back on his heels.

I watch him greedily as he fists his cock and guides the tip to my entrance. We both hold our breaths as he starts to sink into me.

"Townes!" I gasp as he bottoms out inside of me.

"Fuck, I love hearing you say my name like that."

"Make me do it again then," I challenge him, and he grins as he braces his hands on either side of my head and starts to move inside of me.

His lips find mine, and my hands slide over his back, pulling him closer. I want to feel his weight on me. I want to feel every inch of him against me, in me.

We're both so on edge after not being together in a few days, and I know that this first time isn't going to last very long. Already, Townes is starting to lose control.

He starts to pound into me, over and over again, relentlessly. His thrusts push me up the bed little by little. Townes growls, and I force my eyes open to look at him.

"You need a bigger bed," he growls as he shifts his arm to hold me in place, never once slowing his pace inside of me.

I moan, my core clenching around him. I think it's the fact that he's looking out for me and what I need, even when he's equally lost in pleasure, that does it for me.

I'm close. So close.

"Fuck, Mira. Give it to me. Come all over my cock," he orders, and I let go with a cry as I do what he says and come hard.

He grunts and finds his own release, his pace slowing until he stops. We're both breathing hard, and I smile as I look into his blue eyes. His hair is damp and sticking to his forehead, but he's never looked sexier to me.

"Bigger bed," he tells me as he pulls out and tries to get comfortable next to me.

"Oh, I don't know. I kind of like being so close to you."

"We can do that in a king-size bed, too," he points out.

"Alright," I give in, and he lets out a whoop behind me.

"We can go pick one out tomorrow... if you want," he hurries to add, and I smile as I bury my face in his chest.

"If I'm getting a new bed, then there's something that I've always wanted to try with this one," I tell him, and he raises a brow.

"What's that?"

"Fuck me until we break the bedframe."

"Holy shit, I love you," he says, staring at me with wide eyes.

I grin, wrapping my arms around his neck.

"I love you too."

"Now, let's see about making your dream come true," he says as he rolls me under him once again.

It takes a couple of times, but he does make it come true.

Just like I knew he would.

TWELVE

Townes

FIVE YEARS LATER...

"ARE YOU READY FOR TONIGHT?" Xavier asks me
as we finish up work.

"Yeah, I've got it all planned out," I tell him with a grin.
"What about you?"

"Olive wants to stay in, so we're just going to make
dinner together and watch a movie."

"Sounds fun."

"Should be," he says as he gathers up his things and
pulls on his jacket.

"Have fun," he says with a wave as he heads out.

I close the door behind him and then hurry into the
kitchen to check on dinner.

Today is Valentine's Day, and I can't wait to have some
alone time with my wife. Don't get me wrong, I love my son

more than anything, but it's been too long since Mira and I were able to really connect, just the two of us.

Mira and I have been married for four years. We actually got married a year after we started dating, or, I guess, a year and one month since we got married in March. We found out that we were expecting just a few weeks after we got back from our honeymoon, and our son, Noah, was born at the end of January.

We've been a little family of three for the last three years and just recently started trying for baby number two. Mira wanted to wait to make sure we had the hang of this parenting thing before we had any more kids.

I know she was worried that she might be like her mother was with her, but that couldn't be farther from the truth. She's so loving and compassionate. She's never afraid to make a mess with Noah. Seeing the two of them together is so touching. You can see the love between them in every moment, and I know she'll be an equally amazing mother to any other kids we might have.

Mira is still working part-time at Wet and Wild and Shelf Indulgence. She likes hanging out with her friends and making her own money, and I know having that independence is important to her.

She's working at Shelf Indulgence today and took Noah with her. I had offered to watch him here, but he was being extra clingy with her today. Saffron and the rest of the Baker sisters all love him, and they never mind when she brings them into work, though she doesn't usually take him to Wet and Wild.

I glance at the clock as I peek into the oven to check on dinner. I still have at least an hour until Mira and Noah are home and I smile as I turn to get started on our dessert for tonight.

The front door opens, and I freeze, frowning in confusion until I hear Mira call out for me.

"Townes, can you give me a hand?"

I head down the hall to greet her, and my steps quicken when I see Noah looking miserable, standing in all of his winter gear.

"What's wrong, buddy?" I ask him as I kneel to help him take his jacket and boots off.

"He threw up at the bookstore," Mira tells me, and I look up, noticing that she looks a little pale, too.

"How are you feeling?" I ask her as I put his boots and coat away.

"A little nauseous," she admits, and I move to help her take her coat off.

"I'll get Noah. Why don't you go lay down," I encourage her, and she nods, trudging upstairs.

"Do you want something to drink?" I ask my son, and he shakes his head.

"Okay, buddy, let's get you into the bath and then we'll see how you're feeling."

He holds his hands up, and I pick him up and carry him upstairs and into the bathroom. I set him next to the tub as I bend over and get his bath ready. The water starts to fill up the tub, and I pull off Noah's clothes.

His eyes are drooping already, and I know he probably just ate something that didn't agree with him and just needs rest. I hurry to clean him up and get him into clean pajamas. I tuck him in, and he's out before I'm even out of his room.

I pull the door closed a bit, and that's when I hear Mira throwing up in our bathroom. I run into our room and then into the bathroom.

Mira is bent over the toilet, throwing up, and I rush to

gather her hair and pull it out of the way. I rub her back as she throws up again.

"I can run to the store and grab Gatorade or Saltines," I offer, and she wipes her mouth and flushes the toilet. "I didn't hear about any bug going around town."

"It's fine. I'm fine," she says, leaning back against the wall.

"You're not. What do you need, Mira?" I ask her, crouching to look her in the eye.

"Help me stand up," she says, and I grab her hand and pull her to her feet.

I help her over to the bed, and she reaches into her bedside drawer and pulls out a box.

"Happy Valentine's Day," she tells me, and I frown.

"Mira, we can do gifts later. I need to run to the store for you before they close," I argue, and she shakes her head.

"I'm fine. Open the box."

"You're not," I snap, and she smiles.

"Open the box," she says more firmly, and I sit down next to her and take the lid off the box.

I freeze when I see what's inside.

"You're pregnant?" I whisper, and when I turn to look at her, she's grinning at me.

"Yeah. I found out yesterday morning. I have another Valentine's Day gift for you, too, but it's downstairs."

"This is all that I need. You, Noah, and this little peanut," I say, tears stinging the back of my eyes.

"I love you, Townes."

"I love you too, Mira. So much. You, Noah, and our little bean," I say, leaning over and kissing her stomach gently before I scoot closer to her and kiss her too.

"I made us dinner," I whisper against her lips, and she pulls back, covering her mouth like she might throw up.

"Is it the smell? Is it on me?" I ask.

I've been cooking all day, so I'm sure I smell like the Beef Wellington I prepared.

Mira nods, and I back away from her, stripping off my clothes and tossing them in the hamper, then moving the hamper out of the room.

Mira follows me into the bathroom, and I grin at her over my shoulder as I turn on the shower.

"What a weird way to get me to take my clothes off," I joke, and she laughs.

"I'm sneaky like that."

I test the water temperature, and when I turn around, Mira is stripping off her clothes too. I smile softly, holding out my hand to her as we both step into the shower and under the spray.

My hands run over her body, and I kiss her softly as we take turns washing each other. My cock responds to her touch and the sight of her naked body, but I can see that my wife is tired. She can barely keep her eyes open, so I turn off the water and wrap her up in a towel.

She dries off and I lift her into my arms and carry her back to our bed. I tuck her in and kiss her forehead as her eyes droop.

"Do you need anything?" I whisper, and she shakes her head.

"Just sleep," she mumbles, and I nod.

"Get some rest."

She nods, and I kiss her forehead again.

"Happy Valentine's Day," I whisper, and she smiles sleepily up at me.

"Happy Valentine's Day. Sorry that I ruined your plans."

"You couldn't ruin anything, Mira. You gave me the best Valentine's Day yet," I say.

She smiles, her eyes closing, and I tuck her in tighter before I tiptoe out of the room to put dinner away and clean up downstairs.

It isn't how I had planned for tonight to go, but I have my wife, son, and another on the way, so I can't be too disappointed.

I turn off the lights and smile to myself as I head upstairs to my wife.

Looking for more Wolf Valley holiday books? Check out Xavier and Olive's story or read the rest of the Wolf Valley: A Very Grumpy Holiday series!

Don't miss the other Grumpy books! Check out A Very Grumpy Best Friend and the other Wolf Valley Grumps here!

WANT A FREE BOOK?

You can grab Sweets Here.
**Check out my website, www.shawhart.com for
more free books!**

ABOUT THE AUTHOR

CONNECT WITH ME!

If you enjoyed this story, please consider leaving a review on Amazon or any other reader site or blog that you like. Don't forget to recommend it to your other reader friends.

If you want to chat with me, please consider joining my VIP list or connecting with me on one of my Social Media platforms. I love talking with each of my readers. Links below!

<u>Website</u>
<u>Newsletter</u>

<u>Cherry Falls</u>

<u>803 Wishing Lane</u>

<u>1012 Curvy Way</u>

<u>Eye Candy Ink</u>

<u>Atlas</u>

<u>Mischa</u>

<u>Sam</u>

<u>Zeke</u>

<u>Nico</u>

<u>Eye Candy Ink: Second Generation</u>

Ames

Harvey

Rooney

Gray

Ender

Banks

<u>Fallen Peak</u>

A Very Mountain Man Valentine's Day

A Very Mountain Man Halloween

A Very Mountain Man Thanksgiving

A Very Mountain Man Christmas

A Very Mountain Man New Year

Folklore

Kidnapping His Forever

Claiming His Forever

Finding His Forever

Rescuing His Forever

Chasing His Forever

Folklore: The Complete Series

Holiday Hearts

Be Mine

Falling in Love

Holly Jolly Holidays

Love Notes

Signing Off With Love

Care Package Love

Wrong Number, Right Love

Kings Gym

Fighting Fire With Fire

Fighting Tooth and Nail

Fighting Back From Hell

Mine To

Mine to Love

Mine to Protect

Still in the mood for Christmas books?

Stuffing Her Stocking, Mistletoe Kisses, Snowed in For Christmas, Coming Down Her Chimney

Love holiday books? Check out these!

For Better or Worse, Riding His Broomstick, Thankful for His FAKE Girlfriend, His New Year Resolution, Hop Stuff, Taming Her Beast, Hungry For Dash, His Firework

Looking for some OTT love stories?

Her Scottish Savior, Baby Mama, Tempted By My Roommate, Blame It On The Rum, Wild Ride, Always

Looking for a celebrity love story?

Bedroom Eyes, Seducing Archer, Finding Their Rhythm

In the mood for some young love books?

Study Dates, His Forever, My Girl

Some other books by Shaw:

The Billionaire's Bet, Her Guardian Angel, Falling Again, Stealing Her, Dreamboat, Making Her His, Trouble